I0530600

The Adventure

THE RED PLUME PRESS

The Red Plume Press

Petrolia, Ontario, Canada

The Adventure

A novel by

Gerry Van Hoorn

The Adventure

Gerry Van Hoorn

First Print Edition July 2018

Copyright © Gerry Van Hoorn 2018

ISBN: 978-1-7753624-6-3

All characters of this book are fictitious and any resemblance to persons, living or dead, is purely coincidental.

All rights reserved. No part of this book may be reproduced in any form or by electronic or mechanical means - except in the case of brief quotations embodied in articles or reviews - without the prior written permission of the publisher.

Preface

Jim Sevenar, a young man, 24 years of age, was born in the Dutch city of Rotterdam, the largest seaport in Western Europe. He is proud of being a Rotterdammer and would not like to live anywhere else. He did all kinds of part time work in the harbour while he was going to college. The noises and sounds of the ships and tugboats were like a pipe organ to Jim. He lived with his mother who is a widow. Jim's father passed away when he was only 12 years old.

He and his mother lived in a modest apartment in the heart of the city and both had to work to make a living. So, when Jim finished college with the degree of Electrical Technologist (finishing best in his class) he had to find a job as soon as possible to support himself and his mother. Finding a job at that time was very difficult because there was a slowdown in the economy. He found a job as a seaman which he did not anticipate. His mother would be lonely when he was not home for a while, but she understood there was no other way. Jim wasn't sure just how long he would be away from home.

From here on, you can read about the experiences of Jim in this short story, "The Adventure".

Dedication

I dedicate this book to my wife, Mattie Meijer, on the occasion of our 60th wedding anniversary. Life with you, Mattie, has been my greatest adventure!

Chapter 1

After his last effort to find a job in the electrical industry or in construction, which did not work out in a short tim due to a slowdown in the economy, there was only one possibility left for Jim. That was a job as an electrician on board of sea going ship. Jim Sevenar was still young and had no family other than his mother. He grew up as an only child, his father having died when he was only 12 years old.

Jim loved his mother a lot and would have preferred to stay nearby, but money had to be made. He wanted to take care of his mother. He had lots of friends and loved to go to the soccer games of his favorite club, but it was not meant to be for Jim. The job as electrician on board a sea-going ship paid quite well, with free food and accommodation. Jim, with a college diploma, had confidence in himself because he was very qualified in his profession. He loved solving problems in electrical circuits, which was one of his majors in college.

The shipping company where Jim was going to work was new. The ship sailed under a Panamanian flag which was in that time, normal. The shipping company, Hijnen, one of the largest shipping companies in the Netherlands, was looking for a crew. There were, for reasons unknown, not many solicitors for an electrician so Jim was already told that he was hired if he passed his medical examination and his sailor's book was in order. After his medical exam and some little formalities, such as payments and work benefits,

Jim received a letter stating that he was hired and that he should report to the ship as soon as possible.

The only time Jim had sailed was on a ferry to Harris, England. He did not suffer much from sea-sickness at that time. Now he was going to sail on a merchant ship on the ocean. He did not know what the destination of the ship would be or even how long he would be at sea. He knew, though, that it would be for months. Part of his salary would be paid to his mother. Jim did not need much of anything for himself; he was neither a smoker nor a drinker, so it was not much of a burden.

It was a beautiful sunny day, the day when Jim's life started as a sailor.

Chapter 2

Jim was on his way to his new life seaman. He walked along the quay with his duffel bag over his shoulders and his thoughts went out to his new life as a sailor. As a real Rotterdammer, he was quite familiar with the sound of the ports. There were many ships on the quay. Some were being unloaded and others loaded. It was a rush of yuck; there was a busy traffic of trucks and lorries driving up and down the quay. Jim was curious about his ship. In the streetcar on the way to the harbor, he already had some ideas about what was waiting for him.

The ship, which had a real Dutch name, "De Kikker" ("Frog"), was almost at the end of the quay. It was a freighter of an average length, not large but not too small. The ship looked well cared for.

Before Jim went on the gangplank, he saw how everything looked and he observed everything that would come to his good later. When he stepped on board, nobody was there to welcome him. That was strange, Jim thought. There was a sign with an arrow and the words, "Report to the Captain". So, Jim followed the sign and came to the cabin of the Captain. He knocked on the door and from within, a heavy voice said, "Come in." Inside the cabin were the Captain and two other people.

He was received with the question, "Are you the electrician?" When Jim answered the question with, "Yes, I am Jim Sevenar." the Captain said, "Welcome aboard! I hope you understand your job because I do not want to have problems along the way."

He said to one of those present "Carl, you take Jim to his cabin and give him the tour of the ship." When they were on their way to Jim's cabin, Carl introduced himself as the second engineer. With his cap at a jaunty angle on his head, he looked like a jovial man. Jim was a quick study and learned everything about the ship in a short amount of time. It was a motor ship with two diesel engines, two propeller shafts, and a diesel generator for electricity. There was also another small emergency generator for electricity. It all looked neat.

His cabin was small but comfortable. He picked up his belongings, got his bed ready, stepped into his overalls, put on his cap and put his clothes in the closet. His mother had packed some extra things for his health and safety and of course, some cookies and candies for the first couple of days. As soon as he was ready, he left the cabin for an inspection around the ship. Jim made sure he knew where everything was on the ship. He preferred to try out everything that had to do with electrical. The ship would leave two days later and he had time enough to get familiar with things. Carl came to pick him up to show him the workshop and the engine room. There was a store room with some spare parts. Jim learned a lot from Carl in a short time. The crew of the ship consisted of a first (Captain Art Bos) and second mate (Bill Sims), a machinist (Carl Mosman), a cook named Cheng, a Boatsman (Bob de Vries) and four sailors (Fred, Leo, Bas and Edward) and of course, Jim the electrician.

The radio was operated by the second mate. The cabin of Carl Mosman was beside that of Jim. Both men would have a lot to do with each other.

Chapter 3

The ship had a strange load, Jim thought. The cargo consisted of heavy steel frames with different dimensions. It was an advantage that this cargo would be difficult to shift in a storm. Jim did not have much to do with the cargo space of the ship. However, the illumination of the space was his responsibility. The lighting was at the top edge of the cargo area and accessible by a walk way. Carl told Jim that the room had an entrance at the bottom and was only used when necessary.

The ship was scheduled to leave the next morning. Jim made a final inspection to make sure everything was in order. Together with Carl, they got the diesel engines started and the batteries charged. Everything worked fine and both men were satisfied. Tomorrow they would have to get up early because it would be a long, busy day.

The Departure

The engines turned and the captain gave his orders to the boatsman to throw the cables to shore, loose. The sailors turned the winches to roll in all the ropes. The pilot was on board and gave his orders to the tugboat and to the captain.
The engines of the ship only provided some navigation until they were out of port. The pilot then disembarked; the cables to the tugboat and the ship were disconnected. The ship left the sea channel under its own steam. The engines turned at half strength until they were at sea; after that, it was full

power ahead. It was a calm sea with a slight swell. Soon Jim was turned to his first experience at sea.

The sailors were busy pulling down all the ropes to fasten everything that was on deck. The boatsman and the captain checked all of their work. Jim made a final inspection regarding everything that had to do with electricity. The winches were properly covered with lateral covering. The navigation lights and deck lights were already on and everything worked properly. Jim thought to go to Carl and see if he could help him with anything. He went to the machine room downstairs. When he passed the Captain, the Captain asked if everything was in order. Jim replied that, so far, according to his inspection, everything worked properly.

Carl was busy with a temperature meeting when Jim came in. He said to Jim "You are just in time; Jim I need your help." The men were busy working when the cook came into the machine room. He told Jim that something was wrong with his oven. Jim went to the galley with the cook. He saw upon inspection that one of the elements was not working. Jim studied the oven and his attention was drawn to a cable that was plugged in. He saw that something was not right. He unplugged the contact and saw that a wire going in to the oven control box was loose. After a little repair and the cable going back to the oven was plugged in, the oven worked again. The cook was happy, there had to be food cooked for the dinner.

He told Jim that the problem of the oven began with the previous trip and that former electrician did not know what to do with the problem. Jim left a happy cook behind in the kitchen.

Chapter 4

Jim kept his own log and noted everything he had to do every day for work, including repairs. His predecessor certainly did not feel like keeping such records; there was very little known regarding his maintenance and repair work. Jim thought to check his tools in case he needed to use them. He also wanted to inspect the spare parts in the storage room and their logbook for quality. He would also talk to Carl the next day. He wanted to know what had happened on the previous trip out to sea. But first, to put his workshop in order. He had the feeling that there would still be some problems. The day went by quickly and he got hungry. It was almost time for their dinner.

He thought that he had already made a friend with the cook. The food was good and not much was spoken during the meal. Only the second mate told what the news was and discussed the weather forecast for the coming days. The next day, the ship would pass Gibraltar into the Mediterranean Sea on its way to Malaga, Spain where the ship would be loaded with drinking water.

When Jim came to his cabin, Carl hailed, "See you tomorrow Jim, I think I will need your help. Good night".

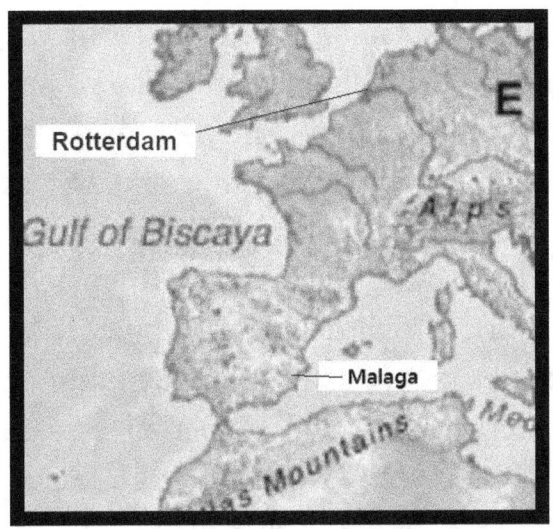

Map courtesy of mapswire.com

Chapter 5

The day began with a friendly sun and a calm sea that was unusual for the Gulf of Biscay. After dinner, it was time for Jim to make his round and to check on everything. He spoke with the boatsman and a few sailors (they all came from Indonesia). The boatsman was not an easy person to deal with. After his round, Jim went to the bridge to tell the Captain that everything was fine and to ask if he had an assignment for him. The Captain said that he was pleased with everything so far. Jim went to the machine room where Carl was working hard. An oil pipe was loose and he struggled to get it fastened. Jim gave him help and when it was done, Carl spoke of his experiences as a seaman. Jim asked Carl if he knew how long the current trip would be or where they were going. Carl answered, "Jim, as far as I know, we are going to Tanzania." But Carl didn't know where they were going after that. He did tell Jim that as long as there was cargo, they would stay out to sea. Jim was disappointed and felt that his mother would be alone and lonely for a longer time than he had anticipated

Carl knew a lot about the electrical profession. Jim would later discover that he could really learn a lot from Carl.

Chapter 6

After having passed Gibraltar, the weather became warmer. Jim loved being up on the deck. He could see the dolphins swimming. He thought of his mother, wondering how she was doing without him. Suddenly, there was a noise that broke his thoughts. It was the boatsman and a sailor who came to him with the gesture, "Come here!" When Jim approached, he was told that the ship had a leak in the cargo area and that there was water in the hold. Jim asked the boatsman why the pumps were not working. The boatsman said that the hoses were already in the cargo space but the pump was not working. Jim was surprised about the problem and went in a hurry to the storage room to get the spare pump. He needed a trolley to get the heavy pump on to the deck. The sailors had to help him to put the pump in to place. When he plugged in the cable and the pump start working. He unplugged the other pump and checked out the cable to the pump. The cable was cut deliberately; he could tell because it was a sharp cut in the cable with no wear or tear. After repairing the cable, the hoses were attached and the cable plugged back in the socket. Both pumps worked hard to pump the water out of the cargo space. Water came into the cargo space with great force. Something had to be done other than only pumping as the ship was taking on too much water. The pumps could not handle this much water coming into the ship for days. Jim told the boatsman that he and Carl would take a look into the cargo space where the water was coming from.

Together, Jim and Carl looked at the drawings of the cargo space and noticed that there was a pipe in the cargo area with a valve for discharging drain water. Carl said to Jim, "We have to go downstairs to check that valve, are you coming?" Jim answered, "Of course Carl."

With tools and water boots on, the men entered the cargo space. They saw that it was not the valve but a leak in the drain water tank. The water was being ejected from the overflow valve in the tank. The valve to send the water to the outside of the ship, however, was open. With much effort and a lot of water on their bodies, they took in the seriousness of the situation and considered what to do about the problem. The water in the cargo space was already 2 feet deep. The tank overflow valve had to be temporarily closed, which was not an easy task. Carl had to go to the storage room to get heavy steel clamps. Before he could step away he slipped and nearly went under the water. Jim grabbed him by the arm and brought him back to his feet. Jim said to Carl, "What if we can't get out of here?" Carl answered "Don't worry Jim, the Lord is with us."

The answer surprised Jim; he did not expect this answer from an old seaman like Carl. When he came back with the steel clamps to close the valve, they bolted them to the edge of the tank. Water was still coming out of the tank but it was not so much. It was an emergency solution for the moment. The installation could not be used until the problem was solved.

Jim was thinking about what could have happened if the cargo had been wood or any other material, they would have been in extreme danger. The steel frames could not move and that made a difference.

Meanwhile, the boatsman had informed the captain about the water in the hold., Carl went back to his cabin to put on dry clothes. Jim felt that something was wrong with the controls to the tank and the drain water valve. He could not let it go and went back to his drawings to see where the electrical power came from.

The electrical control panel was in a small storage space next to the cargo hold. Before returning to the cargo space, he made sure that the electricity was locked to the panel. Together with the boatsman, they followed the cable to the tank and found that the cable was in good condition. The problem could be in the control panel, so Jim went back to the storage room. He opened the electrical panel and immediately saw that the cable was not connected. Jim connected the cable, then inspected the whole installation. Jim put the power back on and went back to the cargo space. He noticed that no more water was leaking now. The outside valve must have closed. For the time being, nothing could not be done.

In the Malaga harbour, everything had to be tested for the functioning of the whole. Jim was not happy with the situation, what would have happened if the problem was not noticed? The idea of shipwreck was not what he anticipated. Another question came to his thoughts, "When and who noticed the water problem in the cargo space? Why did anybody have to be there? Was it just luck?"

Jim told the Captain what was done and that there would be repairs in the harbour at Malaga, Spain. He was not too pleased with the situation but agreed with Jim.

Chapter 7

The next day, Carl was not there for breakfast. Jim went to Carl's cabin and saw that Carl was sick. The cold water of the cargo hold had given him a cold and he had a fever. He could not do his work in the engine room and there was only one Carl trusted and that was the young man, Jim. Carl gave Jim some instructions that he had to pay attention to in the engine room. If there were any problems, he had to warn Carl immediately. Fortunately, everything went well and Jim was able to put Carl at ease. Since Jim was spending his time in the engine room, he made use of the opportunity to take a look at the drawings of the ship. He saw that the valve in the hold was operated pneumatically by solenoid and that the control cable came from the electrical control panel.

Everything seemed to be in order so far, but the risk of trying the installation was too big. Jim started to get suspicious with the way everything had happened; something was wrong and he would talk to Carl about it the next day. But Carl was ill for a whole day. Jim gave Carl some Gravol to ease his stomach, some of the medicine his mother had given to him just in case he got sick on the trip.

Jim was in the engine room when Carl stepped in with the question, "Jim, tell me what is wrong and what do you think is happening?" Jim told Carl what he had done with the control panel, what he had checked and what his findings were. He told Carl that there was something suspicious about all the problems in the cargo area and with the cut cables to the pumps. Carl agreed with him and he said to Jim,

"We must keep everything to ourselves. We need to pay attention to everything that goes on at the ship and make a round in the evening."

Jim agreed with his friend. When he came to his cabin a bit later, he had the feeling that somebody had been inside his cabin. There was some kind of odor in the air that he was not familiar with. When he looked at his desk, he noticed that his desk lamp was still on. He did not use the lamp much. Jim went to his logbook to see if everything was still there. Nothing was out of place, so he did not worry. Jim had a shadow logbook, with more information and his private opinions, which he had stashed away in a secret space. He went to check and see if it was still safe it its secret place, and it was. Maybe he was all wrong. He would tell Carl the next day about his suspicions.

Chapter 8

They arrived in the port city of Malaga in Spain.

Map courtesy of mapswire.com

In the Malaga harbor, they docked at the quay to refill with drinking water. Everything was checked during the loading of drinking water. The waste water system was inspected again and tried out a few times. The drain valve checked out and everything worked fine. Only the valve in the tank was renewed. It was an extra cost for the owner of the ship. Carl and Jim made a tour through the town before they left the next day towards the Suez Canal and Egypt.

On board, Jim and Carl kept an eye out to see if anyone was doing anything suspicious. Leo, one of the sailors, was a strange fellow. He didn't always get along with the other sailors and he didn't talk too much, but the boatsman kept him under control. When Jim was on duty at night, he saw this man always roaming on the deck. Carl had the same experience with this man. Sometimes there was a little fight between the sailors but it always ended in a thrush. Jim got along pretty well with the sailors and sometimes they played a game of cards when there was nothing to do. Later that day, he told Carl about his suspicion that somebody had been in his cabin. Carl told Jim to inspect all the spaces in his cabin every day. He wanted Jim to make sure that no one put drugs or anything else in his cabin. That was probably not the case, but better to check than be sorry. In every harbour there would be a customs inspection and if they find something in your cabin, you are responsible and will be fined or arrested. Jim appreciated the warning from Carl.

They arrived in the port city of Palermo Sicily, Italy.

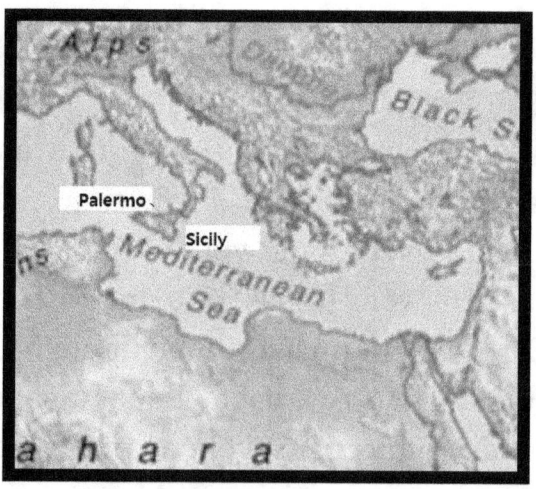

Map courtesy of mapswire.com

The ship docked in Palermo, Sicily for food for the crew and fuel for the ship. The weather was tropical and the heat made it difficult to sleep during the night. Carl told Jim to keep the ports closed. There were vendors with little boats that try to sell all kinds of stuff. Sometimes, these vendors would try to come on the ship by an open port.

At night there was a beautiful sight of the glow of the volcano, "The Edna". They did not go ashore because they had to leave very early in the morning. Their next stop would be the Suez Canal, but first they had to sail another day thru the Mediterranean Sea. Jim enjoyed the beautiful water with so many dolphins sailing alongside the ship during the day and the flying fish at night. It would be another day of tropical heat. For the cook, it was very difficult in the galley. Jim found an old portable fan and after some repairs, he was able to give it to the cook to give him some relief, which was much appreciated.

Jim was thinking about the city of Suez, the Suez Canal and Egypt: he had heard so much about them. He was looking forward to see the ancient history of these places. On his last birthday, his mother gave him a little digital camera and Jim thought he would take lots of pictures on his way.

Chapter 9

Many ships were waiting to enter the Suez Canal at Port Said and when it was finally Jim's ship's turn, it was already midday. Jim took pictures of some of the ships that were waiting to go through the canal. There were two large passenger ships. Jim thought it must be nice to be an electrician on a ship like that.

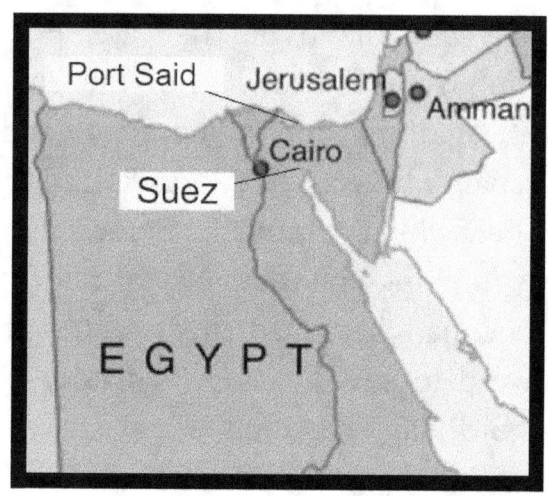

The Suez Canal and Port Said

Sailing through the canal was a disappointment for Jim; the only thing he saw was a few camels along the shore but at least he had the experience being someplace where he never had been. Later, in the port city of Suez, he would go ashore to see more of Egypt. When they docked in the harbour of Suez and were allowed to go on shore, Jim was ready to go. However, Carl told Jim that he was going with him as soon as he was ready. He told Jim not to go by himself because it was too dangerous.

Together they went sightseeing, and Carl told Jim everything he wanted to know about Egypt. It was too short of a visit to see the pyramids but there was much more for them to see and they took a ride on a camel. Jim took lots of pictures to show later to his mother where he had been on his travels. He was happy that he went with Carl because he would not have seen so much or known about everything, especially the camel ride they took. Carl was not only a good mentor but also a good friend, and sometimes like a father to Jim.

Chapter 10

After departing from Suez, they had to sail two days through the Red Sea and the next port of call was Aden in Yemen, a dangerous port to stay in but they needed fuel for the engines. Sailing thru the Red Sea was another experience

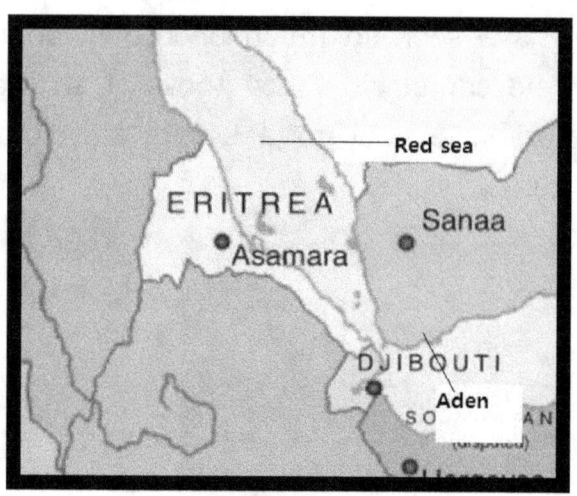

Map courtesy of mapswire.com
Sailing thru the Red Sea

for Jim. First, the extremely hot weather and second, the sheer number of ships coming and going through this body of water. There was not much to do for Jim and he spent much of his time on deck. His daily inspection took less than two hours. Jim took lots of photos of the dolphins that were swimming along the ship. On the second day sailing into the Red Sea, there was another commotion. Jim was called to the radio room. When he entered the radio room, he was told that the little generator for the radio was overheated and had shut down. So, no radio contact could be made.

For Jim, it was another surprise. There was no spare generator and the broken one had to be repaired as soon as possible. Jim did not have any experience with repairing generators but he had to do his work anyway. He took the generator to the engine room work bench and with the help of Carl, they were able to fix the problem. It was another strange coincidence, because it was just a little problem with one of the connections into the generator. It was a surprise that the problem had not earlier appeared. The generator could have been damaged if they had not detected this problem. Jim thought to himself, why is there not a backup system for communications? When all the work was done, both men were exhausted and tired. It was too hot to work but after a shower they were ready for dinner.

The next day they would arrive in the port of Aden, one of the places with much political turmoil. It would be a busy time for Carl and Jim.

They arrived in the port of Aden, Yemen. In the port of Aden, there were lots of vendors coming beside the ship to sell their products. The customs officers came aboard to check the ship's cargo.

After a short stay in the port of Aden, they were going first into the Arabian Sea and after that, into the Indian Ocean where they experienced the worst incident. It was an experience that Jim would never forget and that made a long-lasting impression on the young man.

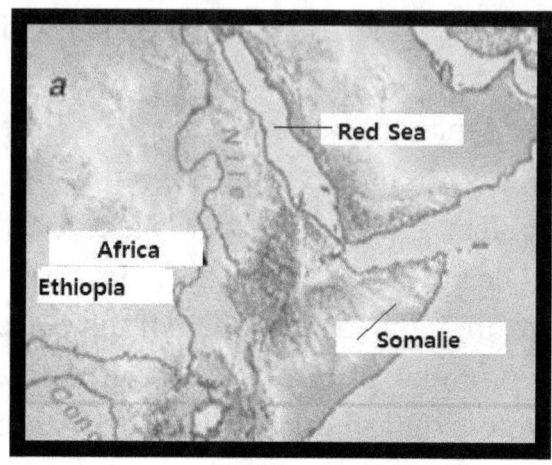

Map courtesy of mapswire.com

The most dangerous place

Chapter 11

Jim was working in the anchor chain room in the bow of the ship when three armed pirates arrived on board. He had heard so much about these capers and the way they took over a ship with violence. Jim went out through a hole when he noticed the pirates because he saw they had weapons. He ducked down and closed the doorway to the chain room. He did not know what to do, so he kept hiding until it was dark enough to be able to leave his hiding spot to go see what was going on. He was not scared but he knew that he was in danger. He prayed to God that he would be spared and that what he was going to do would not put him in danger. Jim had an iron bar with him, the one they used to loosen the anchor chain.

When it was dark enough to take a look over the deck, it was quiet. Fortunately, there was no moonlight and quite dark. Jim crawled past the gang board with the iron rod. When he came close to the deck house, he saw one of the armed pirates with his back to him. He did not understand where he got the courage from later on. Jim stood up and slammed the rod on the pirate's head. (He thought that this hit, no one would survive). The man slumped to his knees. Jim caught hold of him and then laid the man down on the deck. Jim was hiding in a dark part of the deckhouse. The scuffle with the pirate had not made much noise. A few minutes later, Jim was horrified by the opening of the deck house when the second pirate came outside to check on his mate. Jim watched for his chance and hit this man with his rod as well. This man would also not survive, he thought. Jim threw his rod overboard.

He took the weapon of the pirate and did not really know what he would do next. He had to look in the deckhouse. In the deckhouse door was a small window. Jim peered cautiously into the cabin and saw that the crew was being held at gunpoint by a third pirate. He now had to make a dangerous decision. He did not know how to operate the weapon, but he had to act quickly. Jim simply stepped inside and the man turned around, but before he could do anything, Jim struck the man in the face with the butt of the weapon. Carl, not thinking long, immediately took measures and seized the man's weapon. The pirate was overpowered. Jim said to the Captain, "We've taken care of the pirates, change course and turn off all lights of the ship."

The Captain, who was stunned, hurried to the bridge to change the course of the ship and to turn off the navigation lights. The ship had to sail out of the waters of Somalia at full speed. Two sailors were at the bow of the ship as a look out. The pirates were simply put away overboard with weapons and all. The small dinghy of the pirates was cut loose. It would still be a few anxious hours until they were in international waters. Jim and Carl kept watch on the deck. It was a gentle cool night. When the daylight began to break, the Captain praised Jim for his courage and decisiveness and told him to go get some sleep. With all that had happened, the ship had used lots of fuel. All that had transpired with the pirates had to be kept secret. Jim began to realize what he had done, hoping that no problems would arise from his actions. He had killed two men and he suddenly felt very sick. He could not sleep and wished he had not taken this job. He was not a religious person but his mother had taught him about the bible and they always prayed before dinner. Now Jim prayed that he would be forgiven for what he had done. Why did it have to happen this way and that he was not spared from that evil? Finally, he fell in to sleep.

Chapter 12

The ship was back on its original course. It would be a few days before they came into international, reasonably safe waters. The pirates were working off a mother ship, even as far as in the Indian Ocean, so the crew had to be alert every hour of the day. Jim found it hard to believe that something like piracy could exist in this day and age. There should be more protection on the sea to prevent such evil. For instance, navy ships could patrol this area but then again, the pirates were resourceful. He was thinking about the history of piracy in the 17th century. He learned in grade school that at that time they would have punished these countries severely with the destruction of the port city involved in the crime.

The following day, Jim was talking with Carl and asked him what he thought about the whole pirate incident and if he thought there may be some consequences for Jim later. He felt so scared and sorry for what he had done. Why did have to happen to him? Carl said to him, "Jim don't worry so much, we are all in it together; we had to defend our selves against evil." Jim was a little more at ease but it would bother him for a long time.

Chapter 13

When they arrived in the port of Zanzibar Tanzania the ship needed to refuel.

Map courtesy of mapswire.com
In the port of call, Zanzibar, Tanzania.

When they docked in the harbour of Zanzibar, the final destination for our cargo, we were welcomed with a big surprise. As soon the ship was moored, the police came on board and everyone was escorted off the ship. Jim's first thought was that it had something to do with the pirates. The police put the crew in holding rooms and they were not allowed to communicate with each other. Jim was feeling scared and he wished he could talk to Carl but that was not possible for the time. Later that day, the Captain told his shipmates that the police were going though the ship to look for gold. That was a big surprise for Jim and Carl and they did not know what to think about it. Everyone was reasonably treated and they were allowed food and drinks. It was two days before they were allowed to go back aboard the ship. The only person who did not come back aboard was the second mate, Bill Sims. The Captain told us that Bill had informed the Tanzania authorities that there was gold in the steel frames in the cargo. After they had unloaded the ship, they did not find anything. The second mate was arrested and later sent back home at his own expense and we had to wait for another second mate to be flown over from another ship in Suez before we could leave. Carl and Jim knew that all the things that had happened on board the ship could have been done by the second mate Bill but they had no proof of that.

Chapter 14

In the harbour of Zanzibar, they refuelled the ship and took another cargo of copper ore for South Africa, for the port of Shepstone near the city Durban. Before the ship left, the customs officers came on board one more time to check our papers and the cargo. When they were out of the harbour and at sea it was already late afternoon. The cook was in a hurry to make dinner because we were all hungry. There was no conversation about what had happened on board the ship. The new second mate, Jan Baks, was a very young man around 30 years of age. He seemed to be a jovial man. He spoke a little about his previous ship and everything seemed normal. It felt good to have him as a table guest; much better than the previous second mate who did not fit in all that well.

After dinner Jim went on deck to get some fresh air. He was thinking about how long he would be away from his mother and also thinking about what had happened in the last couple of weeks. He was interrupted in his thinking by the new second mate Jan, who asked if he would mind some company. Jim said, "No problem." Jim hoped he didn't ask too many questions about what had happened with the previous second mate, because he did not know the man.

Chapter 15

Sleep had just come to him when Jim woke up with a start to a sound like something had hit the ship. Jim went to the deck to see if anything had happened. He saw Carl who must have had the same idea. They saw a fisher's boat with several men with weapons. Jim thought to himself, here we go again. The captain was already on the railing talking to the man. He threw the rope ladder overboard and one of the men climbed on board. The man was talking to the captain with a calm voice and helpless movements with his hands. The captain called up to the boatsman to lower the anchor to the deck of the fishers' boat. Carl and Jim were watching when the anchor landed on the boat, wondering what was going on.

The men on the boat untied the heavy bolts from the anchor to disconnect it from the anchor chain. Carl said to Jim "What the heck is going on, Jim?" but he did not get an answer. The man who was talking in a friendly manner to the captain gave him a handshake and then left the ship. The fisher's boat sailed away with everybody watching it with the question in their minds of "What happened?"

Later, the captain told Jim and Carl that they needed an anchor and because they had given them one, they would not threaten them. So, it was better to be without an anchor than to have more trouble for everybody. Jim went back to the cabin to sleep. A question came to his mind, was the gold maybe in the anchor? Did they overlook the outside of the ship? Did the second mate, Bill Sims, know more than we thought?

The next day Jim told Carl what he was thinking the night before and surprisingly Carl had had the same thought. It would be a mystery until they were heading home to Rotterdam.

It was a long sail to South Africa and for Jim, the worst was yet to come. After two days in the Indian Ocean, the weather started changing dramatically. A storm was brewing. First the humidity, then the rain. Early in the morning the wind started to increase to wind power 10. The sailors and the boatsman were fastening down everything that could be a problem. Jim made sure that motors on the deck were properly covered. The only problem was the cargo in the hold. The ore was stored in crates and the hold was divided in two spaces. Jim was getting seasick and he was not allowed to go on the deck for fresh air because it was too dangerous. He stayed in the engine room with Carl. The ship was sailing in to heavy gales.

It would be another day before they came close to the city of Dunbar. The ship was as a toy on the waves and the water swelled over the deck. Jim was scared and thought of what all could happen if the ship could not handle force of the storm. Many ships, even larger than their ship, had disappeared in a storm like this. He thought that what happened with the pirates was nothing compared with this storm. Carl saw what was going on with his young friend and told him, "Jim, do you have no faith? Trust in the Lord and nothing will harm you. Do not worry my friend, this will all soon pass."

Jim could not believe the calm and quiet way of his mentor. Later he went to his cabin and fell to his knees to pray that he may see his mother again. He never knew that a man like Carl had so much trust in his faith, and he started to love this man, who acted like he was his father. Early the next morning, the storm quieted down a little bit and the ship laid course again to South Africa. Jim was embarrassed by his childish and scared time during the storm. It was good that he did not know what all had happened in the night during the storm. Lots of things were damaged or blown off the deck. It would be a lot of hard work for Jim in the coming days.

Chapter 16

By now, Jim had been away from home for more than a month and it felt like this ship was his home. There was a lot of repair work to be done. The motors of two winches had to be removed from the deck and that meant taking them down to the workshop. In the work shop, the wires had to be dried and tested so that the wires would not burn down, and that would mean that the motor could not be repaired. There were no spare motors in the storage room. It took many days to do this work and it kept Jim's mind from other things. Several lamps in the light fixtures on the deck had to be replaced as well. The boatsman and the sailors were busy with the repairs of the railing and other things on the ship. The only person who had no extra work besides his daily responsibility was the cook, but he made a special meal for the hard-working crew. The days passed quickly and they were on their way to Durban, port Shepstone in South Africa.

Map courtesy of mapswire.com

In the port of Shepstone (Durban) in South Africa.

Chapter 17

When they arrived in the harbour of Shepstone, it was a pleasant and different view of a harbour than what they had seen before. There were small houses of different colors, like in western Europe. Jim was on the deck and took some photos for his album. His mind was on his mother and what she would think of all the things that had happened since he left home. He felt more secure after the time spent with Carl, who had been such a friend and teacher. Jim believed in the Lord and made Jesus Christ as his Saviour. It made hem feel that there was a definite change in his life. When the ship had been docked and moored and the engines shut down, Carl came to keep Jim company. Both men were watching the busy traffic on the wall. Carl told Jim that he was going ashore to do some shopping because he needed new shoess. He asked, "Would you like to go too?" Jim answered, "Yes, that is a good idea Carl."

A little later, Jan Baks, the second mate came to join them on deck and when he heard that they were going ashore, he asked if it was ok for him to go with them. They had accepted Jan as a friend a few days ago when they were at the dinner table and had talked about religion. Jan was a good man, not because what he stood for, but by the way he acted to the other men aboard.

When they had had there lunch and freshened up, the three men went ashore. They would have liked to go to the city of Durban, but the small city of Shepstone looked so friendly and so quiet. They were taken in by the little stores.

Carl found a cobbler store and bought a nice pair of shoes. Jim bought a colorful table cloth and a beautiful vase for his mother. For himself, he and bought a new pair of pants and some souveniers. It was one of the most cozy times Jim could think of since they had left the port of Rotterdam.

When they came back aboard the ship, the cargo had already been removed. There was no other shipment known. The first thing on the mind of the captain was to get a new anchor for the ship. There was not much in the way of ship repair or storage place in the harbour of Shepstone, but as a wonder they found an anchor and brought it to the ship. The boatsman and the sailors then attached it to the ship's anchor chain.

The next day they were going to Cape Town to pick up another cargo and that meant going around Cape Good Hope, a dangerous part of the sea, especially without a load. The sea was always rough in that area. Jim did not know about this so he went to sleep that night without worry on his mind. When he woke up the next day, the sky was cloudy and it was a rainy day but luckily, no storm. The next day the ship experienced a little rougher weather but it was not a storm, so they could stay on course. By the end of the afternoon, they arrived at Cape Town where they had to wait before they could go into the harbour. This town was much larger and much busier than the towns before. Many ships were docked and there was lots of traffic on the quay. The ship could not stay too long in the harbour and so the loading had to go fast. The new cargo was sandstone for Cabon and the port of Ibrrefill, a two day's sail. They left the harbour early in the morning with a calm sea. The boatsman and the sailors had the day off because they had worked overtime the day before. We're going in the direction of home, thought Jim. Luckily, they did not have to sail back through the Indian Ocean. Everything on the ship worked fine, giving them more time to relax.

Jim was thinking about what he would do when he got home again; would he go to sail on a ship or try to find a job on shore? He would miss Carl, who was not only a good friend but also like an older brother, but he didn't want to think about that yet. He would be happy to see his mother again. After dinner, Jim went up on the deck to relax and to have some fresh air. The sea was calm and there was not much traffic, only an oiltanker going in the same direction. As the sky got darker, one could see the phosphorous glow of the waves. To be a sailor was not such a bad life after all, thought Jim.

Chapter 18

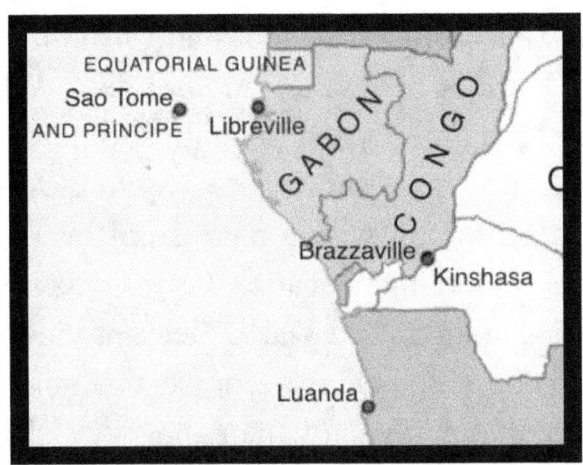

Map courtesy of mapswire.com

The harbour of the City of Libreville was different again from the other ports they had visited so far. A completely different culture from what was on the east coast of South Africa. The captain told the crew that if they were going ashore it was at their own risk. There was some trouble in the country of Cabon. The port of Libreville was protected by the Cabon army. They had to unload very quickly. The ship was inspected by the Cabon customs for weapons. The language in Cabon is French so the crew could not understand much. The customs officers did not find anything. Fortunately, they were able to buy some fuel for the ship. The cook could not leave to go to get some food. There was no new load for the cargo space so the captain contacted, via the radio, the ship's owner for directions. The new destination was Freetown, Sierra Leone on the west coast of Africa. There the ship had to pick up a load of carbon and special rolls of paper products for Casablanca, Morocco. The ship had to sail without a load and that was not good for the company. The weather was not that great either, so the ship had to sail without ballast for another day. When they were on the Great Atlantic Ocean on course to the Atlantic Ocean, they met a Dutch navy ship on its way to the Netherlands. It was nice to sail along with a navy ship for a while. It gave Jim some good feelings because the sea was rough. Luckily, the sun was shining and it was a pleasant view on the ocean. Pretty soon the ship will set course to home, Jim thought. The night fell quickly and then the navy ship was out of sight.

HNS The Zeven Provincien

Second mate Jan was on the radio when Carl came into the station for an update of the weather. Jan asked, "Carl what is on your mind? I can see that something is bothering you." But Carl didn't answer the question. Instead he'd said, "I'd like to know the weather forecast for the coming days." Jan told him that the weather was looking good. When Carl was gone, Jan took another look at the news to make sure he was not lying.

Later, when they were getting close to Freetown, Jan went to the engine room and found Carl and Jim working on the emergency generator. In a jovial tone he asked, "How are you guys doing?" The answer was, "Jan, we are almost out of fuel for the engines and we do not know if we will make it to the harbour of Freetown."

Jan said, "Don't worry, we can always call upon the navy because the HMS Zeven Provincien is in the port."

The look on the faces of Carl and Jim told of the load that had just lifted from their shoulders. A few hours later, when they were in the harbour of Sierra Leone, they were right out of fuel. They were lucky to have made it that far. They had used the fuel from the emergency generator to fuel the engines.

In the harbour of Freetown, Sierra Leone.

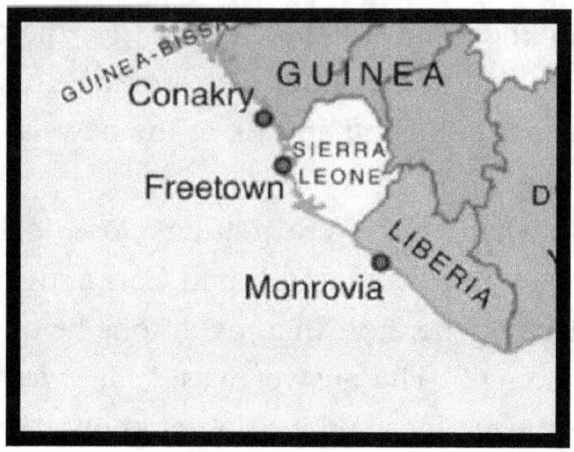

Map courtesy of mapswire.com

Chapter 19

The harbour of Freetown was larger than Jim expected. On the quay it was there was more traffic than he'd seen before. The navy vessel, the HMS Zeven Provincien was on the same side of the harbour and close to the "Kikker". As soon as the ship was docked, some of the navy sailors came to take a look along the quay. Some of these sailors were girls. Later, when Jim went ashore to do some sightseeing and shopping with Carl, they met some of the navy girls. One of these girls was from Rotterdam and Jim was very interested in talking to her. Jim thought she was very pretty. She told Jim that they have been in an exercise with other nations and that they were now going home. All went so fast and before they departed to the ship, Jim had the address, telephone number and name of this girl called Betsie. Carl was amused with his friend and made some funny remarks that made Jim blush a bit in embarrassment. Carl said to Jim, "First love, Jim? You better be good."

The next day, the navy ship left and Jim was on the deck to wave to whomever was looking, hoping that one was Betsie. The boatsman and the sailors were very busy with the loading of the ship. The carbon was in thick plastic bags and the paper in large rolls. It all had to be stored separately, by dividers. The hold had to be dry and the load had to be stored one foot off the floor. The work took almost the whole day. Then the ship needed fuel, drinking water and food. The cook was very happy because not much was left in the way of supplies. Everyone pitched in to buy some extra fruit and vegetables. It was late that night before the ship was all set to sail for morning.

Chapter 20

The night was cool so Jim had the port open, but he could not sleep. He was thinking of his meeting with Betsie. He was not ready for a relationship and would he ever see her again? The moon was shining bright and Jim closed the port just in case he could not sleep with the moonlight. He fell in a deep sleep and was dreaming about the beautiful navy girl Betsie that he had met.

On their way to Casablanca, Morocco

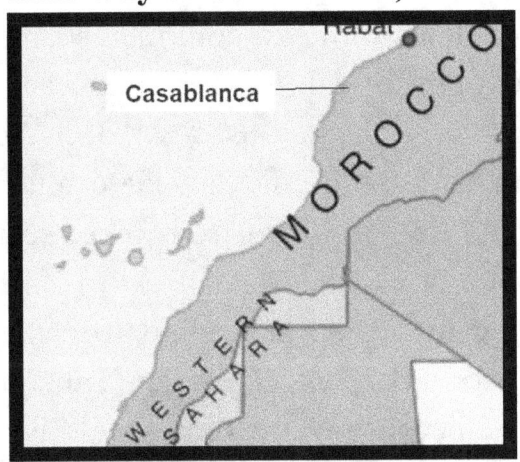

Map courtesy of mapswire.com

Cheng the cook woke Jim with a knock at the cabin door. Jim had overslept the alarm and was missed at the breakfest table. Cheng brought Jim a few sandwiches and a cup of coffee. He said, "Jimmy, man not eat, no good." Jim thanked Cheng and hurried into his clothes. He ate the sandwiches and then drank the coffee in a hurry because he had to be in the engine room with Carl. The ship was leaving in a hour. When Carl saw Jim he said, laughing, " Dreaming about Betsie?" Jim got a color on his cheeks and did not know what to say. The engines were already turning and the ship was moving away from the wall, commanded by the pilot and a tugboat directed the ship out of the harbour. Jim was thinking of the pleasant time he had and the way everything went. He was not thinking of the bad experiences of his time at sea. He went to the deck to see if everything was going right. The winches operated perfectly and before they jnew it, they were in full sea. Their was a light gale but the sky looked dark; there was a storm brewing. Jan, the second mate, joined him and both men shared some thoughts about the next port of call. Casablanca was not a town to go shopping; it was a dangerous city. Jim did not anticipate going ashore because he did not have much money left to buy things and he had heard from other seamen that it was not a pleasant city.

Later that night, the gale winds became stronger but it was not the storm they expected. The captain was concerned about the load because wet carbon would be worthless and a loss for the company. It took two days to reach the Casablanca harbour. Everything with the load had gone well. The pilot of Casablanca came on board and it was night before we were docked.

To Jim's surprise, the Dutch navy ship was also in the harbour. His heart was beating faster with the thought of Betsie.

Jim had an idea and he went to Jan with the question, "Jan, do you think you can send a message to the Zeven

Provincien?" Jan answered, "Why do I have to send a message to that navy ship, Jim? Oh, I know. You want to know how that little navy girl is doing, right?" Jim was blushing in his face and said, "Of course, Jan. I like her." Jan asked Jim what the message would be and turned on the radio. They contacted the navy vessel and sent the requested message. To the surprise of both men, there came an answer right away. It was the operator of the ship with the question, "Is Jim there? Here is Betsie"." Jan told Jim that he could talk a little bit with his girl friend. After a few minutes, they had to close the coversation. Betsie told Jim that they had to leave early in the morning. She said, "See you again, Jim'. This was music to Jim's ears and it made him feel so good. He said, "Thanks Jan. I am so happy."

When he woke up the next morning the navy ship was gone. It was back to reality for Jim but could not get his mind off the girl.

Chapter 21

The unloading of the cargo went without incident and the new destination would be Bordeaux, France. The captain contacted the owner of the ship and was told that there was a new cargo coming. They had to wait for a freighter from Tindouf, which was carrying a load of glass-sand with the destination Bordeaux, France. The next day in the late afternoon, trucks brought the cargo that was stored in big steel drums. It took a long time to bring the cargo on board because it needed a special crane. When it all was on board, the customs officers came to inspect the ship. Finally, early the next day, they left the harbour on their way to Bordeaux. Jim thought hopefully that is was the last stop on the way back to the Netherlands.

On their way to Bordeaux, France

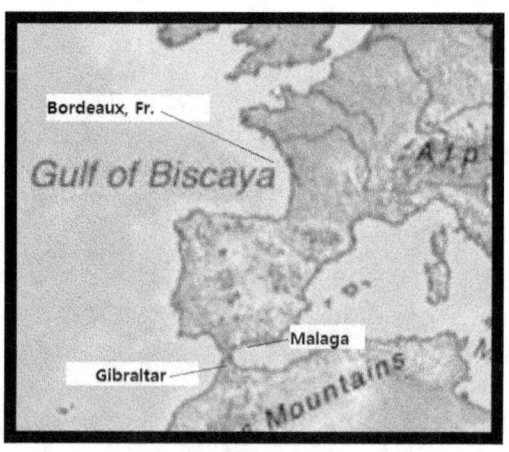

Map courtesy of mapswire.com

The idea that they were getting so close to home made Jim very happy. He not only thought about his mother but now he was also thinking about Betsie. Jim wrote his mother a letter every time they were in a harbour, or he had sent a postcard. This time he wrote a letter to both Betsie and his mother to tell them that he was looking forward to seeing them again. Jim had no idea that the last part of the trip would not be easy.

Chapter 22

When Jim woke up, it sounded like the ship was hitting something. He quickly stepped into his coveralls and went to the deck. There was a heavy storm; the ship's bow was in the waves. Jim thought, why did it have to be such bad weather when they were so close to home? He went for breakfast to join Jan. Jan said, "Jim, we are in for some bad weather." Jim was not feeling good and after a few sandwiches, he went to see Carl. When he came into the engine room, Carl was looking concerned and told Jim to stay off the deck and to stay down in the engine room with him. The storm was only the beginning of a larger gale. The ship had a heavy ballast with the cargo in the hold, which was properly stored. Luckily, it could not move from one side to the other. Carl told Jim, "Jimmy my friend, we have to pray because this will be the most dangerous part of our trip." Carl handed Jim a life jacket and told him to put it on just in case they had to leave the ship. Both men went on their knees and prayed for their salvation.

In the communication room, Jan had to stay on the radio just in case there came a may- day call. He heard that other ships were out in the storm. He was thinking of his wife, Elly. He had been lucky on the trips he had made before, always with a safe return. Would it this time different? He pushed the thought away.

The boatsman and the sailors were not allowed on the deck either, because the captain had warned them to keep all the watertight doors closed, to check that all the ports were closed and to wear life-jackets all the time. The captain and Jan kept close contact. So far, the ship could handle sailing on the stormy waves.

After a few hours, they reached the Gulf of Biscay and it was getting darker and it started to rain. T here were a few may-days on the radio and that meant that ships were in trouble. The captain laid course to Bordeaux and put on his life-jacket. The only thing that could go wrong was the fallout of the diesel engines. He asked Jan, "Jan, is there any change in the weather?" and told him to wear his life-jacket. Captain Art, an old sailor that he was, did not worry to much. As long he kept his ship on the waves, they would make it.

In the engine room, Carl and Jim kept a close eye on everything that was turning and moving. The ship was bouncing up and down and sometimes the propellers of the ship came above water. This was the dangerous part, to control the engines. The captain had told Carl to keep them on half speed for the time being. Jim had the emergency generator running just in case the electricity should fail.

Jim asked Carl, "What would happen if we have to leave the ship in an emergency? Can the lifeboat handle all of the crew?" Carl said that he never had been in that situation before but he hoped it would not come to that. Again, Jim was surprised with the calmness of his mentor and friend. What is it to have so much faith and trust in God? Was he not scared? The bouncing and shuddering of the ship started to get worse.

Both men had to hold themselves to the workbench. Jim thought on all that had happened on the ship since he had been on it and wondered if it was some kind of bad luck streak.

The time passed by slowly and then all of a sudden, it was quiet. It was like the ship lay in the harbour. Then it started bunging again. The telephone rang and it was the captain.

"Carl, put the engines on full speed. We are going to make or break it, there is a tornado brewing and we have to et to the harbour!"

The engines at full speed were fighting to turn the propellers. Carl looked at Jim and said, "Jimmy, we are going to make it. I know old Art; he is at his best when in trouble." Two rough hours passed by and they finally made it to the harbour at Bordeaux. A sigh of relief came from the mouth of Jim and before he knew it, he said, "Thank you, Lord!" Carl looked at him with a smile.

Bordeaux is a large harbour with many different loading areas. Their cargo of drums of glass-sand was to be delivered on a special unloading dock. It took a while before they were moored. The ship unloaded the cargo without any incident.

A load for Rotterdam was already waiting on another part of the harbour. The ship had to be towed to that area and it was getting late in the evening. They had to wait till the next day to load the cargo. Jim thought, that is just fine, because the weather did not change too much.

Carl told Jim to inspect the batteries for the diesel engines to make sure that they would not have too much trouble with starting the engines the next morning. The fuel for the ship was already in the tanks. They were fully loaded and had enough to get to Rotterdam.

The new cargo was delivered and ready to hoist into the hold. The shipment was carton boxes with bottles of wine in large crates. The boatsman and the sailors were busy storing the crates securely so they could not move. Carl thought that this was a very special shipment which he had never seen before. He was sure that it must be for a very special occasion in the Netherlands. The captain, the boatsman and the sailors inspected everything on the ship. Art, the captain, wanted to arrive safely in Rotterdam. He was thinking of the luck they had making it into the Bordeaux harbour. He would be happy to go home without any more problems.

On their way to Rotterdam, The Netherlands

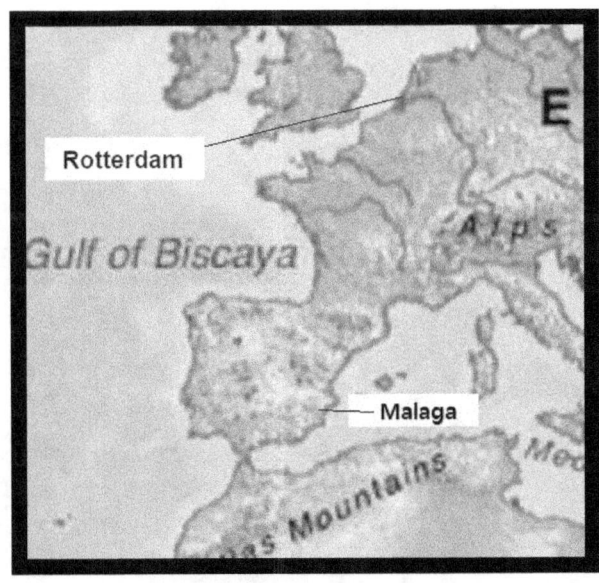

Map courtesy of mapswire.com

Chapter 23

The next morning, Art gave the order to start the engines. The start up went perfectly and the engines were turning idle until the ship was out of the harbour of Bordeaux. The pilot was on board to maneuver through the many ships in the harbour. The weather was much better but still the sea churned with large waves. The ship was on its way for the last destination, which was home.

They sailed through the Gulf of Biscay, which was rough until they came into the North Sea canal. From there the ship had a much calmer ride. Jim was on the deck when Carl came up for a break and some fresh air. The weather was getting warmer and the sun came out from the cloudy sky. Jim told Carl that he would miss him and that he had learned a lot, not only about his job but also the Lord Jesus Christ. He gave Carl a hand and said, "Thank you Carl, for being a big brother and friend." Carl replied, "Come here" and gave Jim a big hug.

The last sail took a little more time than Jim thought. Jim knew that when you are waiting for something, it always seems to take a long time. He had already cleaned his cabin and packed his clothes. He made sure that everything in his cabin was in good order. He did not forget to pack his private journal.

While at the harbour of Bordeaux, Jan, Carl and Jim had exchanged their home addresses so that they could stay in touch with each other.

Home sweet home

Jim handed over his journal to Captain Art Bos and told him that he wished him good luck for the future. Art replied, "Jim, it was a pleasure to have you on my ship and whenever you want to come back, please let me know. I will also give the best reference for your future job." Jim said, "Thanks Captain!" and went on his way to get his duffel bag from the cabin. He met the boatsman and one of the sailors and with a handshake, they said good bye.

On his way, he met Cheng the cook, who gave Jim a big hug with the words, "Jimmy, friend, good man." He turned his head so that Jim not could see that he had tears in his eyes. Jim answered, "Cheng, you are the best cook in the world and I will miss you."

Walking over the quay on his way home, he took one more look at the ship, his home for the last three months. He had left in early March and now it was June. Next month would be his birthday. Jim had to go first through the customs office before he could leave the harbour to catch the streetcar to go home. Clearing customs was not difficult for him because he had nothing to declare.

In the streetcar, he was thinking about his mother. He had already telephoned her and she knew he was on his way. She sounded so happy and relieved that he finally was coming home. When Jim got to the house, he pushed the doorbell and his mother must have been behind the door because the door went open immediately.

His mother looked at him and then she gave him the biggest hug a son could wish for. The tears rolled over his mother's face and she said, "Jim, I am so happy you are home safe! Go the living room I will make you coffee and I think you would like a piece of apple tart, too."

Jim left his duffel bag in the corridor and went into the living room where he had a very big surprise that almost made his heart explode. In a chair in the living room was a beautiful looking, red haired girl with curls, Betsie.

Jim thought, how is this possible, but then he lost no time to take her in his arms and said "Oh Betsie, I love you so much!" Betsie replied, "I love you too, Jim."

When his mother came in the room with coffee and cake they both told her what had happened and when they had met each other, far away from home.

Betsie told Jim that she was on leave from the navy. She would be at home until this coming Friday, but she was coming home again the next Saturday. Her time in the navy was over and she was going to resign to take a job on the wall. Jim was happy about her decision; he was also going to try again for a job away from the sea. They were all talking about the things they had experienced.

The future for Jim looked bright and he was going to meet Betsie's parents the next week. Jim brought Betsie to the streetcar, gave her a big kiss and said, "I love you, Betsie and I cannot wait to see you again."

Jim had an extra week's pay so he could stay with his mother to relax and to tell her all about his adventure as a sailor. He also told her about Carl and his faith and that he would like to go to church from now on.   His mother was happy with her son because he became such a good man.

Epilogue

A year later Betsie and Jim became engaged and were married shortly after. Carl was Jim's best man. Jim found a good job as a technologist with a large electrical design company and Betsie worked in the local hospital.

They rented a house with extra rooms for future children and Jim's mother.

The Mystery

The story about the anchor of the ship was still a mystery. The funny thing was that Jim's wedding present from Carl was a small golden anchor with the words' Hope Faith Love'. Both men became friends for life.

Two years later, when Carl attended the dedication of the son of Jim and Betsie, he told Jim about the rumor about the mystery of the anchor of the ship. The story was that some men who worked on the ship before it was commissioned had put an anchor on the ship that was made of gold. Later, these men were overheard by a sailor in a bar, where they were drinking, about the destination of the gold. The sailor did not know about the anchor. He later told the story to the second mate, Bill Sims.

When Carl retired and left the seaman's life, he told Jim that the strange things that happened on the ship were still a mystery. Captain Art Bos had informed the owners of the ship as to what had happened and they were going to investigate.

So, this is the end of the story,
"The Adventure".

General Map 1

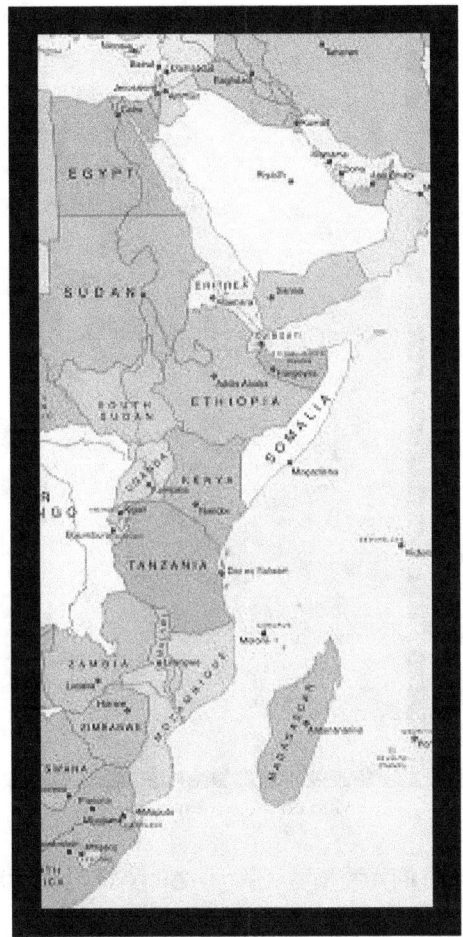

Map courtesy of mapswire.com

**The beginning of the travel from Rotterdam,
The Netherlands to an unknown future for Jim.**

General map 2

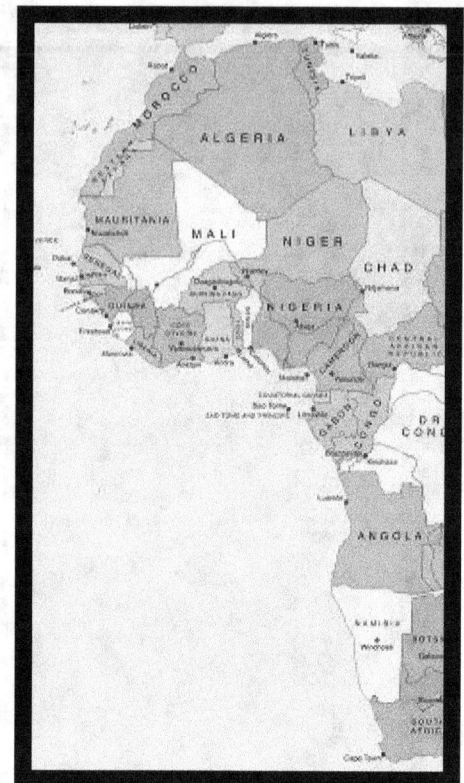

Map courtesy of mapswire.com

On our way home to Rotterdam

www.ingramcontent.com/pod-product-compliance
Lightning Source LLC
Chambersburg PA
CBHW071207130626
46555CB00004B/1614